THE BAPTISM

Also by Shelia P. Moses

The Legend of Buddy Bush
National Book Award finalist
A Coretta Scott King Author Honor recipient

*I, Dred Scott: A Fictional Slave Narrative Based
on the Life and Legal Precedent
of Dred Scott*

The Return of Buddy Bush

Margaret K. McElderry Books

THE BAPTISM

shelia p. moses

Aladdin Paperbacks
New York London Toronto Sydney

ALADDIN PAPERBACKS

An imprint of Simon & Schuster Children's Publishing Division

1230 Avenue of the Americas, New York, NY 10020

Copyright © 2007 by Shelia P. Moses

All rights reserved, including the right of reproduction in whole or in part in any form.

ALADDIN PAPERBACKS and related logo are registered trademarks of
Simon & Schuster, Inc.

Also available in a Margaret K. McElderry Books hardcover edition.

Designed by Debra Sfetsios

The text of this book was set in Fairfield.

Manufactured in the United States of America

First Aladdin Paperbacks edition June 2008

2 4 6 8 10 9 7 5 3 1

The Library of Congress has cataloged the hardcover edition as follows:

Moses, Shelia P.

The baptism / Shelia P. Moses

p. cm.

Summary: In twentieth-century Occoneechee Neck, North Carolina—an area still affected by its history of slavery—twelve-year-old Leon Curry reflects about whether he wants to give up sinning to be baptized alongside his twin brother.

ISBN-13: 978-1-4169-0671-1 (hc)

ISBN-10: 1-4169-0671-1 (hc)

[1. Twins—Fiction. 2. Baptism—Fiction. 3. Family life—North Carolina—Fiction.
4. African Americans—Fiction. 5. Slavery—Fiction. 6. North Carolina—History—20th
century—Fiction.] I. Title.

PZ7.M8475Bap 2007

[Fic]—dc22

2005028408

ISBN-13: 978-1-4169-5833-8 (pbk)

ISBN-10: 1-4169-5833-9 (pbk)

This book is dedicated to William S. Creecy Jr.
(July 19, 1913–August 5, 2005), who served as principal
of W. S. Creecy School for thirty-six years.

He raised an entire village.

Contents

Sunday
1

Monday
37

Tuesday
55

Wednesday
79

Thursday
91

Friday
99

Saturday
109

Sunday
119

Author's Note
132

Acknowledgments
134

THE BAPTISM

Sunday

TODAY IS SUNDAY. The only day of the week that we don't have to work in the fields. The only day we get to wear our nice, nice clothes. We do not have church this Sunday, so Ma said we can go fishing. We have fishing clothes just like we got Sunday go-to-meeting clothes. There will be no fishing next Sunday morning, because me and my twin brother Luke Curry will get baptized. We ain't saved or nothing like that. We just doing what our ma, Lemuel Curry, telling us that she wants us to do. What she calls the "Christian" thing to do. She says if that ain't reason enough for us to want to get baptized, then we best remember that she is the one who puts the food on the table in the old house where we live. She says for us to remember that she wash the clothes that we wear to church, school, and everywhere else. The clothes that she buys with money she gets for washing and ironing clothes for white folks. Money she gets for baking and walking all over town to sell her baked goods to anybody that got some money. Ma said she wash the sheets that we sleep on. In the house that she pays the rent. If all of that ain't enough, she says to think about the old oak tree in the backyard. On that tree there are many limbs. On the limbs there are many small branches that make perfect switches. She cuts three at a time. First she cuts them, then she braids them, and those switches can make you remember anything that you have forgotten.

When she finishes all her braiding, she

yells, "All right, twins, these switches got your names written all over them." Now, that really ain't Christian-like at all, but me and Twin Luke get the point. We will do as she tells us as long as we live in her house back here in the Occoneechee Neck. This is the house that me and Luke were born in. The white folks who own these Neck houses don't care nothing about us or the house we live in. Oh, but the land, well, that's a different story. See, they own the land, too, and they take care of the land because that's how they make their money. That's just the way it is in the Neck.

The Occoneechee Neck is as strange as it sounds. "Occoneechee" is an Indian name that means "powerful river." Now, long before the white folks came and took the land, the Indians lived back here. White folks took the place the Indians called home and turned it into cotton plantations, including the Wells plantation that we live on now. The Vernona plantation that was once owned by General Matt Ransom is right down the road. I reckon Matt Ransom is as famous as anyone in these parts will ever get. White folks around here talk about him like he was a god. During the Civil War, when white folks didn't want slavery to end in the South, he fought Yankee Colonel S. P. Shear and his army from the North, at Boone's Mill down the road. It was there that Matt Ransom and his soldiers turned Colonel Shear and his Yankee troops around after a three-hour bloodbath. Matt Ransom and his boys could not let the Yankees into this county because they were coming to blow up the railroad over in Seaboard. The railroad that was bringing General Robert E. Lee, his Southern troops, and their guns to Northampton County to help Matt Ransom keep slavery alive and well. In other words, Matt Ransom kept my grandma and all her kin as slaves a while longer, after the big fight at Boone's Mill.

After slavery Ma said that poor colored folks sharecropped because they didn't have no place to go.

All these years later, ain't much changed. We still work for white folks and take their orders all day. At night we go home and Ma tells us what to do. But she loves us and they don't.

Ma says that the way white folks treat us ain't going to last always. She says a change is going to come, and until then, God will take care of us. But she says in order for God to take care of us, we got to do right.

Right by Ma means, "You twins are twelve now and it's time to get baptized."

Yes, we had our birthday last month on the Fourth of July and we turned twelve. See, when you turn twelve in Occoneechee Neck, everything changes. You get to do stuff that you couldn't do when you were eleven.

I knew that this was going to happen because our cousin Pattie Mae Sheals that live about five miles from here over on Rehobeth Road told us what happened to her older brother and sister when they turned twelve back in the thirties. And she knows what's getting ready to happen to her. Like us, she knew that when you are eleven, you can't say the word "lie," you can't sit on the front porch with grown folks, and the boys can't go fishing with the men. But most of all, you can't get baptized. It's a big thing to turn twelve and go down in the water and come up saved. Saved to the point that you can't lie anymore. Saved to the point that sinning is behind you.

I don't know about Twin Luke and Pattie Mae, but sinning is fine with me. For all I know, sinning don't hurt nobody but the sinner himself. So why do I have to go and get saved?

Being a sinner bothers the grown folks more than it bothers me. Grown folks like my ma and all the saved folks around Northampton

County. Especially the Neck people feel you have to be saved. These folks think that life is really better after you go down in the water. After ole Reverend Webb at Branches Chapel screams the word "Hallelujah" over you while half drowning you, he says, "I baptize you in the name of the Father, the Son, and the Holy Ghost." If you ask me, one time in the water is not going to change nobody. But that is what they believe and that is what my grandma, Bessie Curry on my daddy's side, says will do the job to get us to heaven.

I figure I have six days to sin all I want to. Luke got six days too, if he will go along with the plan. We also got six days to get the devil out of us. But I reckon ain't much devil in Twin Luke, because he is Mr. Goody Two-Shoes most of the time. Me, I'm going to do all my sinning first and then I will pray for the Lord to forgive me. I will ask him to move Satan out of my life for good. I will tell Twin Luke to do the same thing if he feels he need to, and then we will be born again.

Maybe getting baptized won't be too bad. Miss Mary Lee, who is Ma's friend that live over in Ahoskie, is definitely going to give me and Twin Luke some candy like she give all the children at Branches Chapel after they go down in the water in the river behind Branches Chapel. Ma says Miss Mary Lee been giving children candy for years. She says she gave her candy when she got baptized many, many years ago. I will appreciate the candy, but I am going to miss sinning some kind of bad. Sinning is the main reason I get out of bed in the morning. It is the reason that I wake Twin Luke up too. He ain't no everyday sinner like me, but every now and then I can get him to throw a rock or two. He really tries to be a good boy, but sinning is surely in his blood, if he will just accept it. I know it is, because sometimes he just join in with me and we get to doing some mess around here sho'nough.

Now don't get me wrong, we twins don't do

any major, major sinning like stealing. Just stuff Ma would take our skin off for if she ever knew about it. We lie when we need to. That's a sin. We take stuff like an extra cookie out of the jar if we want to. That's a sin. We beat up kids because they white. That's a sin. But the biggest sin that we do is to our big brother, Joe. Me and Twin Luke call him Joe Nasty because he don't like to take a bath every day like Ma make us do.

Getting Joe Nasty in trouble any way that we can is worth every whipping that we get. We do that because he gets us in trouble, then act like he don't know what is going on. Ma says we better leave Joe Nasty alone and stop all the mess we doing wrong. I ain't leaving Joe Nasty alone for all the money in Northampton County. Joe Nasty just spoiled because he the oldest, and Twin Luke spoiled because he came out of Ma after I did and she say he is the baby. So I am the middle child and I don't get any respect around here. Sometimes I kind of feel adopted. Ma says, "How can you be adopted boy and you an identical twin?" She says for me to stop talking crazy and tell God that I am sorry before we go down in the water next Sunday. But I ain't sorry and she don't care about how I feel no way. She has never asked me if I was sorry for my sinning ways. She just knows we are going to stop sinning and we are going to stop this week.

Ma should have asked Twin Luke and me if we wanted to get saved. She ain't asked, and she says she just talks to God and God said, "Yes, it's time, and it is time on Sunday." She first mentioned us going to the mornin' bench to get baptized when we had our birthday party last month. Right after cake and ice cream from Kennedy's dime store in Jackson she made the big announcement, and she ain't stop talking about it since then.

And she reminding us again right now as she yells down the Roanoke River bank where me and Twin Luke are trying to fish in peace.

"Come in the house, children, it's time for lunch!"

The Sundays when we don't have church, Ma lets us fish till lunchtime. We don't have church every Sunday because each of the four colored folks' churches in the county meet twice a month.

I ask Ma, "Why colored folks have church twice a month and white folks have church every Sunday?" and she said she will tell me when I get baptized. Forget that! I didn't want to wait for no baptizing, so I went to Grandma Curry and she told me the reason. She said that it ain't but three colored preachers in Northampton County, so they rotate from church to church. Grandma says that one day we will have enough preachers around here and we can have church every Sunday morning. I never told Ma that Grandma Curry told me this. But I went to Ma one more time last week and asked her why we have to get baptized now.

"Twin Leon, you and your little brother is twelve now and you getting baptized next Sunday morning because I said so. Now, that's the last time you get to ask without me cutting three branches."

But this morning she yelling down the riverbank about lunch and the mornin' bench because we ain't walking fast enough for her.

"Twin Luke, Twin Leon, put them fishing rods down and come in this house after you wash your hands. We need to talk about next Sunday morning."

Talk about next Sunday morning for what? Like she said, it ain't nothing to talk about, since she done made up her mind already that we're going to the mornin' bench.

I have two problems with Ma. First, she keep on calling Twin Luke my little brother because he popped out of the oven two minutes after I did; but he ain't my little brother.

The second problem I have with Ma is

she's always letting us do something fine, like fishing on Sundays, and then she start yelling for us to come in the house.

Well, maybe I got three problems with Ma. Ma let Joe Nasty do just as he pleases when he pleases. All of us have to stay home from school during cotton season in early fall to help do the picking. But Joe Nasty don't go to school when it ain't cropping season. He just stopped coming and Ma ain't said a word. Ma didn't make Joe Nasty get baptized until he was good and ready. He did not get good and ready until he was sixteen. He is seventeen now, so he only been saved for one year. And he still just as mean as a rattlesnake.

If anybody in this family needed to get baptized at twelve, it was Joe Nasty. I don't know why Ma didn't force him into the water a long time ago like she doing us. I think it had something to do with our daddy Joe Curry dying.

Us twins was little when Daddy died, but

I remember him. Joe Nasty looks so much like Daddy that Ma could hardly look at him when he first died. He is tall with red hair and yellow skin like Daddy had. Now Joe Nasty ain't as strong as Daddy, and he was not old enough to be the man of the house when he died. From what I remember, things kind of fell apart around here after Daddy met his maker. And Ma couldn't make Joe Nasty do nothing. He is mean. God forbid, if anything ever happens to Joe Nasty and he dies the sinner that I know he really is, he would go straight to hell. He almost went last year. I thought for sure my big brother was on his way to an early grave. What happened is funny, now that I think about it.

Joe Nasty is always playing tricks on Twin Luke and me, and the last one of his not-so-funny tricks almost got him killed. He was still playing cowboys and Indians as late as last summer, when he almost killed himself. One day when Twin Luke and me were playing, Joe Nasty just came out to the barn and said he was a better cowboy than us. Mr. Know-It-All said he could tie a rope better than Twin Luke and me.

We didn't care then about his rope and we don't care now, but he wouldn't listen when we told him to go away and leave us alone. Before we could tell him for the third time that we didn't care, he had tied a rope way up in the barn loft.

"I bet you won't stick your head in it," I yelled from down below. Joe Nasty ain't scared of nothing, so he put his head in that rope and pulled it tight. He was laughing and laughing, until he lost his balance and slipped from the floor of the barn loft. There he was, hanging from the barn like a real dead cowboy. Twin Luke and me thought that was pretty funny until we saw his eyes roll back in his head.

"Oh, Lord, I think he done hung himself," Twin Luke cried out.

It was no time for crying, as I climbed the

old broken ladder to the top of the barn. Joe Nasty had been some kind of mean to us, but I didn't want him to die. And I sho' didn't want to listen to Ma hollering and crying like she had done at our daddy's funeral. So I cut that rope with my pocketknife that Ma don't know I have. The one I got out of the pocket of Daddy's overalls that Ma left hanging on the hook in the pantry for a year after Daddy died. Down Joe Nasty fell from the barn loft. Headfirst!

"Is he dead?" Twin Luke asked in between his baby tears, as I ran down to check on our brother.

"He ain't dead, because I can see his heart beating through his shirt. But I best get Ma."

I touched his heart, and surely enough he was still alive. But he had a big knot on his head.

"Twin Luke, you stay here while I get Ma and Mr. Frank."

Mr. Frank is Ma's husband. We call him

"Filthy Frank" behind his back, because he don't take as many baths as Joe Nasty do. Ma is a clean woman, but she married him anyway. She probably didn't know he don't take many baths. She said she loved our daddy, but she got married again two years after he died so that we would all have a new daddy. I was fine with having a dead daddy, thank you very much.

When I reached the house, Ma and Filthy Frank were sitting on the front porch. Sitting there like newlyweds. He was holding Ma's hand like they just got married yesterday. Filthy Frank use to make me sick when he first married Ma. He still do.

"Ma, y'all better come to the barn quick. Joe Nasty is 'bout dead."

"'Bout dead!" Ma yelled as she ran off the porch. Filthy Frank followed Ma with his old self. He is too old for my ma. And he doesn't smell good. He just short and fat. Daddy was tall and lean. I still think about how good

Daddy and Ma looked together. Ma is tall and beautiful. She can make any man look good, except Filthy Frank.

When we all got back to the barn, Joe Nasty was still knocked out cold, but not dead. His head looked bigger than it was when I left, and his light skin was getting darker.

"Get the car, Frank!" Ma yelled.

It would be three days before Joe Nasty came home from the hospital over in Rocky Mount. Ma said it would take her three years to pay his hospital bill. He know Ma don't have no "get well" insurance, so he should stop doing stupid stuff. Stupid stuff that cost Ma money. Ma says the relief worker ain't going to pay for him being a fool. They pay for stuff like colds and stomach pains. Ma says they going to cut her relief off soon anyway, because she have a husband. They keep saying it going to end, but it don't. I guess they let her keep getting relief insurance because white folks like Ma and they know

Filthy Frank ain't no good. But it ain't going to last forever.

When Joe Nasty came home from the hospital, he said he saw God when he fell from that barn loft. Grandma Curry said, "He lying. He ain't seen God, he saw death."

Revival was a week away when he came home from the hospital, so Joe Nasty said he was going to the mornin' bench, and he wanted to get baptized. Sure enough, that Monday night when Reverend Webb opened the doors of the church for anyone who wanted to be saved, Joe Nasty went down front while Miss Kisseye was hymning, "Have you been baptized?"

Reverend Webb was finishing up his sermon when he saw my sinning brother coming down front, and he said, "The doors of this church are now open. If there is anyone who is not saved, let them come and come now. Give your life to God."

Joe Nasty could have waited until the end

of that week, but he didn't want to. He didn't wait because the almost-hanging scared the soup out of him. Grandma Curry was right. He ain't seen God, he saw death.

Being saved did not last with Joe Nasty but one week. He was throwing rocks at Twin Luke and me by Friday and cussing like a sailor by Saturday. By Monday he was chasing girls up and down the tobacco fields. When he caught them, he tried to kiss them on the mouth. Knowing all of that, why should I get baptized? Twin Luke and me ain't ready to stop throwing rocks, and we still cuss when ain't no grown folks around. Well, ain't no need to lie on Twin Luke; I do the cussing.

And what about kissing the girls when we get older? We can't give that up. We just starting to know what to do when we catch them in the tobacco fields. You kiss them and run. Why would Ma want to take all that good sinning away from us?

The least Ma can do is let us make up our own mind. The least she can do is tell us face-to-face why she got to do everything that folks in the Neck do. Why she got to yell at us like she doing right now.

"Did y'all hear me tell you to come in this house?"

Twin Luke starts running up to the house from the riverbank, because he ain't nothing but a mama's boy. I hope Ma don't die before he do, because I would not be a twin anymore. Twin Luke would die the same day if we lost Ma. I really do not think he would live a minute on this earth without her.

I ain't running nowhere. If I have to get saved, I am going to do wrong as long as I can. Luke is already home and done washed his hands. I did not even start to walk fast until I started smelling Ma's blackberry dumplings. Can't nobody from the Neck to New York make dumplings like my ma can. She can cook the best everything, but dumplings is what she cooks better than anything else. It's her best dish because before Filthy Frank came here, we ate dumplings almost every day. Not because we liked it, but because it was the cheapest meal Ma could make. Joe Nasty picked the blackberries, and flour is cheap. Ma saved the blueberries for her customers, because they harder to find than the blackberries.

The other thing Ma's blackberry dumplings did for us was it kept our bellies full through the night. After Ma married Filthy Frank, he claimed we did not have to eat dumplings anymore. But now we have dumplings for lunch and dinner.

Filthy Frank brought groceries home from Mr. White's store on Fridays for a while. That was fine at first, but I got tired of Filthy Frank quickly and I started to miss our daily dumplings. It did not help much when Mr. White saw Ma at the fabric store when he was buying fabric for his wife, and he told Ma that Filthy Frank owed him sixty whole dollars for groceries Mr. White let him have on credit. I was with Ma and I remember the look of shame on her face. Poor Ma had to help Filthy Frank pay Mr. White that money back.

Mr. White didn't know him that well because he was from Rich Square, not Jackson, where the Neck is.

He didn't know that he couldn't trust Filthy Frank.

The only reason Mr. White let Filthy Frank have food on credit in the first place was because Daddy used to do the fitting around the store. And Ma been baking for Mr. and Miss White at Christmas for years. Filthy Frank got a car, so why didn't he just ride back over to Rich Square to Mr. Wilson's store where people know him? Heck, I know why. He probably owed him, too. Ma is so smart about everything but Filthy Frank.

"Ma, lunch is good," I say, trying not to look at Filthy Frank, who wants us to call him Daddy.

I ain't calling him Daddy nowhere, no time, nohow. My daddy is dead and that's the only man that will ever hear the word "daddy" from my lips. My daddy wouldn't go around running up credit to sixty dollars. What made it so bad was Filthy Frank was getting the groceries on payday like he was paying for it with his weekly paycheck. Ma should have asked him what he was doing with his money if he was not buying food. My daddy would have never lied to Ma.

Daddy was a good man with bad luck. Luck so bad that he died at forty years old. Well, he didn't die. He was murdered. Ma said it was an accident, because that is what helps her to sleep at night. But colored folks around the Neck say a white man named Mr. Bennie Pollard, who lived across the Roanoke River from us, murdered Daddy in cold blood. And they say that the sheriff should have arrested Mr. Pollard if he thought he killed my daddy. But he did not. So the sheriff just as guilty of killing my daddy as Bennie Pollard. All I know is that it was snowing one evening when Daddy drove his old pickup truck into Jackson to get some food before it got too bad outside. He wrapped up real good and kissed all of us good-bye. That was the last time we saw Daddy alive. The snow fell and fell and we waited and waited. We waited for our daddy to come home to us. We waited all night.

The next morning they found Daddy's truck three miles down the riverbank with Daddy frozen inside. Poor Daddy still had his cigarette in his mouth. We never heard his truck come down the path that leads to the river, so that told everybody with good sense that he did not try to come home on this side of the riverbank. Mr. White at the grocery store said that Daddy had never showed up there for no groceries. He had known Daddy all his life and he would have remembered if he came in the store. I believe Mr. White, because Ma said that Daddy only had ten dollars in his pocket when he left home and he still had ten dollars when they thawed out his wallet. Colored folks said they believe Daddy was killed by Mr. Pollard because he owed Daddy fifteen dollars for three weeks of ditch digging.

So I believe Daddy needed his money and he went to Mr. Pollard and told him so. Mr. Pollard ain't nothing but poor white trash that's always trying to get coloreds to work for him like the rich white folks do. I believe he didn't have the money and Daddy made him mad when he went there asking for the fifteen dollars. Mr. Pollard's wife left him for a man over in Murfreesboro a while back, so no one was home to see him kill my daddy. They said Daddy had a big hole in the back of his head from the crash. But I think Mr. Pollard hit him in the back of the head as soon as he turned his back.

They said Daddy's cigarette was tight in his mouth, like he had lockjaw. I think Mr. Pollard hit my poor daddy so hard that he bite down on that cigarette in pain. Poor Daddy! God knows that Daddy stopped at that man's house on the way to the store. That was why Daddy's truck was on the other side of the river and not near us. If so much snow wasn't coming down when he left home, they could have proven that from looking at the tire tracks.

It was almost Christmas and Ma always liked a nice new piece of fabric for Christmas. Daddy would have asked for his money a thousand times to get that fabric to make Ma happy.

This is what I know for sure: When I am older, saved or not, I am going to catch Mr. Pollard out at the fishing pond and find out the truth about what happened to my daddy.

Joe Nasty caught him out at the pond one day last spring and pulled a cotton bag over his head and whipped him real good. Mr. Pollard ran into town and told the white sheriff that he knew it was Joe Nasty who beat him up. Mr. Pollard keep forgetting that he ain't nothing but poor white trash and them white town people don't care if Joe Nasty beat him, but he can't kill him. He keeps forgetting that he ain't got no money. But the sheriff pretended that he cared and picked Joe Nasty up for questioning, and then he let him go. If Mr. Pollard was one of them fine white folks like the Barnes, Ransoms, or Wells families that own half of the Neck, Joe Nasty would be as dead as our daddy.

You can't mess with these fine white folks and get away with it. Last year Daddy's cousin and Pattie Mae's uncle, Buddy Bush, almost got himself killed over a white woman who said he tried to rape her. He lived in Rich

Square on Rehobeth Road with the people who raised him before all that mess happen to him. They're nice people, Mr. Braxton, who died last fall, and Miss Babe Jones.

They arrested Cousin Buddy and put him in jail long enough for the Klan to break him out to hang him. Cousin Buddy got away from them and made it North with some help from the school principal, Mr. Creecy, and my daddy's blood kinfolks that live over in Rich Square. They are black Masons. But Cousin Buddy had to leave Northampton County to stay alive. So I know good and well they would have done something to Joe Nasty if Mr. Pollard was a white man with money. Maybe they wouldn't have killed him, but they would have made Joe Nasty wish he was dead.

Ma could not take losing Joe Nasty, too.

Ma went to Daddy's funeral and cried so bad that Reverend Webb never got to preach his sermon. He just told the choir to sing and he let Ma cry until she could not cry anymore. When the choir started singing "Precious Lord," Ma got worse with her hollering. That was Daddy's favorite song.

Finally Reverend Webb just told them to stop and he turned the service over to the black undertaker, Joe Gordon. He tried to keep Daddy's casket open so that the folks from up North could see his body because they had gotten to town so late. We had been looking at him all week while he lay dead in our living room. Ma would not let Mr. Gordon take the casket to the funeral home, like colored folks had started to do. Mr. Gordon usually kept the body in the funeral parlor until the night before the funeral. Then he would bring the dead folks back to where they use to live for one night.

But not Daddy. Ma wanted him with her as long as she could. Even after Daddy's dead body was in the living room a whole week, Ma still did not want to bury him.

Not even after the funeral. Poor Mr. Gordon finally closed the casket after Ma almost pulled Daddy out.

After that they had to drag Ma out of the church to the grave site. She went kicking and screaming until she finally fainted. That was a good thing, because she would have never let them put Daddy in the cold ground if she was conscious. Grandma Curry carried on bad too, but not like Ma. That's the only time in our lives that Ma didn't put us first. Grief had Ma that day, and I don't think she even remembered that she had children. Grandma Curry cared for us until Ma could not cry anymore. It took her about two months to stop all the crying. Then one morning she woke up and said, "Children, Daddy ain't coming home. We got to find a way to make out without him. I am going back to washing for the white folks, and you all got to work for Arthur Wells Jr. when it is time to pick the 'bacco and the cotton. Sometimes you might have to miss school." I knew Ma was in bad spirits when she started talking about us staying out of school. She always sent us to W. S. Creecy School in Rich Square on the bus that came by for the colored children.

I hope Ma's heart ain't never broke like that again.

Ma was so sad that she got baptized again. She said she needed to renew her religion so that she wouldn't believe that Mr. Pollard killed Daddy. Grandma Curry didn't get baptized; she got her a Smith & Wesson. A gun that she said belongs to her and Mr. Pollard if she ever found out he really killed her only child. Joe Nasty remembers some stuff from that sad time that we twins don't remember. He said that one day Grandma Curry caught Mr. Pollard walking down at the riverbank and she walked up to him.

"Bennie Pollard, I am Joe Curry Sr. mama. I try to be a good Christian woman, but if I ever find out you killed my boy, you can't hide under your mammy's coattail from me." Joe Nasty said our grandma turned and walked away from Mr. Pollard like she didn't care if he shot her first. She had said what she had to say.

Ma ain't that kind of woman. She ain't said a word to Mr. Pollard from that day to this one. Ma needed religion. That was the third time that she got baptized. First she got baptized when her ma, Grandma Ella, who is dead now, told her to at twelve. Then she got baptized after she and Daddy was sinning in the barn and she got full of baby with Joe Nasty. The folks said she was a sinner and needed her soul cleaned as soon as the baby was born. Daddy said that was fine and good for them, but Ma needed his love and not some more water on her face. So Daddy married Ma and loved her until the day he died.

One time in the water is enough for Twin

Luke and me. I am going to get baptized Sunday and that will be the end of that.

Maybe after I get baptized I will like Filthy Frank the way Twin Luke does. But I ain't never calling him Daddy, and I better never catch Twin Luke, who is on his third bowl of blackberry dumplings, calling him Daddy either.

I close my ears while Twin Luke is talking nice to Filthy Frank.

"Mr. Frank, are you coming to watch us go down in the water come Sunday?"

"Sure, son, I will be there." Then Filthy Frank looks at me. I look down into my bowl. Ma's dumplings sho' is good.

2

MONDAY

GROWING UP IN THE NECK means one of two things. Your grandparents owned slaves or your grandparents were slaves. One or the other.

For us it meant both.

Ma and all her children are half-white, and our grandma on Ma's side was Sir Arthur Wells Sr. slave woman. The land in the Neck that Matt Ransom and the Barnes family did not own, Arthur Wells did. And he owned the slaves that Matt Ransom and the Barneses did not own. My grandma Ella Wells was his slave, and he had five children with her during and after slavery. Ma was born long after slavery was over. She was the last born, and she had a twin name Lucille, who died at birth.

Ma might as well been dead too, as far as her white daddy was concerned. Ole Man Wells, who died many years ago, ain't never owned up that he was my ma's daddy. He ain't never owned up that he had five children with my grandma and that he had other children all over the Neck. Children who somehow saved enough money to move out of the Neck and away from the Wells family, so they would not have to live in shame. Ma is the only one of his colored children that still lives back here. Three of them, Uncle Fish, Uncle Malachai, and Aunt Bee, live over in Woodland. The oldest child, Uncle Henry, saved enough money and moved to Harlem, New York. Harlem where Cousin Buddy is. And he changed his last name to Bush, because he said he wasn't no Wells. He said he ain't no Bush, but he ain't a Wells, either. Uncle Henry say that Cousin Buddy made him proud to be a colored man because he was smart enough to get away from the white folks who tried to kill him, so Bush was a better name for him.

Grandma Ella hated it when they talked about Ole Man Wells. She died when she was real old and rarely put his name in her mouth, according to Ma. When she did, she called him "that man." Ma said she remember how he would come to the house and have his way with Grandma Ella until her boys got big and she think Ole Man Wells thought they would come in there and kill him. Now, she didn't tell me this. Ma told Miss Babe Jones, and Pattie Mae, who ain't nothing but an easedropper, overheard them and she told me. She said that she heard Ma telling Miss Babe that all Ole Man Wells did was keep Grandma from ever marrying anyone and kept her full of his babies. He even made her use his last name all of her life. He made all the Neck people that lived on his land use his name, even when slavery was over. Folks say if he found out you were using another last name he would make you move off his land. He did not care if you could pick a bale of cotton every day, he would kick you out for not following his rules. He wanted you to do as he told you. Some of the men would change their name just so he would make them move. But the women, like Grandma Ella, had no place to go.

According to Pattie Mae, all of Ole Man Wells's other children by different women moved away from Northampton County. I don't know if that is so, because the Neck is filled with half-white Negroes and they all look like the white folks that live back here. They don't know who is whose daddy.

I need to get baptized, because just

thinking about Ole Man Wells makes me want to go out to his grave under the old oak tree and dig him up and tell him a piece of my mind.

It is bad enough that we live in this house, but he is buried here. His son Arthur Jr. owns the land and the houses now.

We rent the house for fifteen dollars a month. Joe Nasty says he only charge Ma fifteen dollars because he know in his heart that Ma is his sister. He looks just like Ma, except he has no hair on his head. I don't know for the life of me how he can know Ma is his sister and still treat her like he do. But the truth be told, he treat her better than he do anybody else back here.

Filthy Frank claims he is going to move us out of this Neck next year because he is tired of Ma's half brother Arthur Jr. We will see about that. Filthy Frank always talking big about what he going to do. I think he is going to do what he been doing since he married Ma: nothing!

A year from now Ma will still be washing white folks' clothes to help make ends meet, and Filthy Frank will still be working wherever he can find work. Right now that would be the chicken house. A year from now we will still be going to school off and on because we have to work for Mr. Arthur. Every Monday for the last month we start our week just like we are doing today, priming this tobacco. This is what we will do until twelve noon on Saturday.

I want to go back to school every day, not just when we ain't working. I can't do that until the chopping is done in the Neck. Then we can go to school with the other children, until cotton picking time.

Pattie Mae says she gets to go to school every day. Her and her ma, Mer Sheals, live in the white folks' house, but Miss Babe got her own land and if Miss Mer get too tired of the white folks, she can always go up to Jones Property and live with Miss Babe. It's nice to have what Ma calls options. We ain't got no options like Pattie Mae. Maybe one day I'll go to Shaw University over in Raleigh like the people who started Creecy School did. Mr. W. S. Creecy Sr., who is dead now, started what used to be Creecy Institute long before I was born. It used to be called The Schoolhouse at Willow Church, then it was called Rich Square School, until they changed it to W. S. Creecy long before W. S. Creecy Sr. died in 1940. Now his son, W. S. Creecy Jr., is the principal. Older people call him Spence, but we better not ever let Ma hear us call him that. Ma told me and Twin Luke that anyone that is old enough to be our daddy or mama, we better call Mr. and Miss.

I sure do like that Mr. Creecy. He and all his sisters and brothers went to college and now they are schoolteachers. Me and Twin Luke want to be teachers too. Ma has promised us that this is the last year we are staying out of school to work in the fields, even if she has to work night and day. She said she hate that she let Joe Nasty ever stop going to school. Ma said that one day we will be teachers too. Just like the Creecys.

I believe Ma, because she ain't never lied to us. Lie like Filthy Frank does. I would love to wake up next August on a Monday morning and not have to go to the 'bacco field like we in right now.

I hate these fields. One of the main reasons I hate 'bacco is because of who just walked up. It's Mr. Arthur's boy, Arthur III. He ain't priming no 'bacco, he just come out here to look at us colored folks work.

"Be nice," Twin Luke says, before I can say a word to my first cousin. The white cousin.

"'Be nice'? What do you mean be nice? I ain't thinking about White Cousin."

Twin Luke looking all crazy. "You need

to be nice because we getting baptized on Sunday and that means no sinning this week. Picking on our white cousin is a sin, Twin Leon, it's just a sin."

White Cousin don't even speak. He just turns his head the other way and chews on his tobacco like he always does. He ain't old enough to be chewing on no tobacco, but he does whatever he wants whenever he wants to. He can act any way he want to, because as much as I hate it, he got our blood running in his veins. He thinks he is so special, but I know that he know that lily-white rich granddaddy was my granddaddy too. Not that I wanted him to be my granddaddy.

So he don't have to speak, but his granddaddy made this mess, not me, not Twin Luke, and not Joe Nasty.

Joe Nasty ain't going to let him get away with not speaking.

"Cat got your tongue, White Cousin?" He says it just like that! Joe Nasty the only one of us that got the nerve to call White Cousin "White Cousin" to his face.

White Cousin don't even look at my big brother.

"You hear me talking to you, White Cousin?"

White Cousin mad now.

"I ain't your cousin, colored boy."

"'Colored boy'! Is that what you just called me?"

"That's right. You colored and you a boy. Now, what you going to do about it?"

Joe Nasty looked at me like I just picked this fight.

"Now, Leon, which one of you twins going to beat White Cousin for me? I am too old and I might hurt him. So one of you got to do the job. One of you got to beat White Cousin and teach him a lesson."

Twin Luke never stopped pulling the 'bacco leaves off the vine. He ain't trying to fight nobody for nothing. He ain't like Joe Nasty and me, so I know I am the one who gots to get White Cousin. I decide not to beat him. Instead I take a vine of poison ivy and run him down. When I catch him, I have a time rubbing him down with the poison ivy.

"Stop, colored twin!" White Cousin shouts as I rub him from head to toe. I ain't trying to hurt him too bad. Just want to make him feel that poison ivy for a few minutes.

When White Cousin starts to turn red, I let him go and get back to work. He runs like a rabbit. I know he going to tell his daddy, my white uncle.

Look at Twin Luke. He mad at me for messing with White Cousin. "You know, Leon, we ain't going to be able to go sit on the mornin' bench tonight. As sure as you are standing here, White Cousin going to tell on us."

Twin Luke look so sad while he talking to me. He really is a good twin when he ain't hanging around me. Maybe I should leave him be and let him be the good person he trying to be. If White Cousin gets us in trouble, so be it. If he comes back out here I will give him some more.

I know he going to tell his rich daddy and his rich daddy is going to tell Ma. But I can live with that. White Cousin got poison ivy, and that's worth never going to the mornin' bench.

It's twelve o'clock. Lunchtime. I don't want to go to the house, but I am so hungry. I know we in big trouble, Joe Nasty and me. I might as well get this over with.

Ma is waiting for me when I open the back door.

"Don't you two sit at this table," Ma says when I walk into the kitchen. "Sit on the porch by yourselves. Arthur Jr. been up here and he said you been messing with his boy again and that boy got hives all over his body. Why do you keep messing with that boy?"

"You mean White Cousin?"

"Shut up! Leon, that boy is not your cousin.

He don't own you, so why you own him? Let that boy be. Let the past be."

I don't say another word because Ma is ready to get a knife and cut three branches from the old oak tree.

I hate that tree. It is the key to all my whippings. It is also the final resting place for Ma's daddy, Arthur Wells Sr. I wish they would move his body from under the tree and bury him at their fine white house at the end of the road. His wife, Miss Rose, who must be one hundred years old now, probably don't want him buried there, neither. Pattie Mae told me that Miss Wells know all about her husband having a bunch of half-white children all over the county. She probably glad that she don't have to look at his grave every time she look out of her window. It's a shame that we have to look at it every day. Poor Grandma Ella and Daddy were taken over to the colored folks' cemetery when they met their maker. Ma should think about how she goes to that tree to get branches to beat her children. That man under that tree is the reason we in the mess we in to start with.

You know, I bet he laughing in his grave at all this mess he done caused. God-fearing colored folks sitting around waiting to get their justice from the Almighty after they get to Heaven, but Ma is beating me because I want to get a little justice right now.

Right now Ma is two seconds from cutting the switches and braid them real tight like she braids our cousin Gayle's hair. She don't care about the history of that tree. When she done with braiding the switches, she will start punishing me and Joe Nasty.

"Lord, maybe I shouldn't have beat White Cousin after all." Ma is tired of our mess. Now Ma looking at me; then she looks at Joe Nasty.

"Joe, go around back and cut me three long switches and braid them for me. I am tired of Twin Leon's mess."

Three? What is she talking about? She needs six so that she can beat him, too. He the one who told me to get White Cousin; now he ain't even going to save me from Ma? I can't believe that White Cousin didn't tell his Pa 'bout Joe Nasty starting this whole mess.

Filthy Frank is looking at me like he all crazy and mad at me. But he better not put his hands on me. He shouldn't be here, anyway. If he got so much money, then why he come home every day for lunch? He should buy his lunch like other men or take a bag of food with him. I don't like him and he knows it. He ain't really done nothing to me. I just can't stand the thought of him sleeping in Daddy's bed. He probably kisses my ma late at night while we sleeping. *Kiss on, Filthy Frank, but you best not hit me*, I think as I bend over for Ma to do what Filthy Frank probably would give a million dollars to do.

"How many times are you going to hit me, Ma?"

"How many times did you rub poison ivy on Arthur Jr.'s boy?"

"I don't know, Ma, maybe once or twice." That lie made it worse.

Lord, Twin Luke crying louder than I am.

Joe Nasty probably in the back room, laughing. I just know he is. That's all right, because he got the devil in him and I know he will get another whipping sooner or later.

After Ma is done whipping me, she make me sit on the porch with no lunch, while everyone else eats leftovers from last night. Then she send us back to the 'bacco field.

Ma don't even mention us sinners going to the mornin' bench tonight.

TUESDAY

IT'S TUESDAY MORNING, and Ma fussed all night about White Cousin. But I know he needed to be taught a lesson. He thinks he is going to treat me like his granddaddy treated my grandma. He thinks he going to treat me like his daddy treats my ma. But he is wrong about all of that mess. So maybe I didn't go to the mornin' bench last night, but I will be good and go tonight. We didn't even go to church last night. While lying in bed, I hear Ma telling Filthy Frank that gas cost money and we ain't going every night this week. She says we will go two or three nights like we always do. And we sho' ain't going after I been acting like a fool all day. I will just have to stay out of trouble so that Twin Luke and me can get this thing over with. He acts like it's the end of the world if we don't go to the mornin' bench. He just kissing up to Ma so that she will know he is a good boy.

Ma mad at me, and I can hear it in her voice.

"Leon, get out of that bed and get some water for the washing before you go to the 'bacco field today!"

This is a house that don't need no walls, the way Ma yell from room to room.

I get my sore behind out of the bed, and guess who is already at the pump getting water? Twin Luke!

"What you out here so early for? You ain't the one who got to pump water."

"I just want to help you, Leon. If you're good today, we can go to church tonight and go to the mornin' bench. I don't want to drag out this getting saved all week. Don't you want to get this over with?"

"Guess I do," I say to Twin Luke so that he won't cry again. "Ain't no need to rush with pumping this water. It's going to rain and Ma ain't going to be able to wash, and we don't have to go to the 'bacco fields."

God sho' does answer prayers. As soon as the words come out of my mouth, the sky falls in. We grab the bucket that is only half-full of water, and run into the house.

Ma is in the kitchen, cooking us a big breakfast because Miss Bertha paid her for washing last week. Extra money means extra meals. Filthy Frank drinking coffee like he is so important. Like he paid for it. When I told Grandma Curry how late Filthy Frank sleeps, she said that my daddy always said, "A farm man that ain't up and out of the house by five o'clock ain't doing much." It's seven o'clock and Filthy Frank is still here just like he is every morning. He better take his pretending self to work. He changes jobs every six months. He was working at the meat house, but now he's down at the chicken farm plucking chickens. What in the world Ma marry a chicken plucker for? My daddy had his own business doing different work for white folks and colored folks that could afford to pay him. And he worked on his own time. If he needed to be up early to keep his word with one of his customers, then he was up. If he needed to be out late, then he did that too, and then he was on to the next job he could find. He said he did his own work so that his children would never have to work for the white man like we do now. We worked with our daddy when we could work. He had a lot of odd jobs for us to do.

And we got paid, too! Most importantly, we went to school every day. We didn't start this staying out of school mess until Daddy died. Ma just don't have options. If Daddy had lived, he would have saved us enough money to get us off of this old plantation farm by now. That's all he talked about. He had saved a little money under the bed mattress, but Ma had to use it to pay the undertaker after Daddy was murdered. It was still not enough, and the folks around here dropped money in a hat at the door every night before the funeral to help Ma out. Daddy was hardworking and folks knew it. They wanted to help us.

Now I got to look at this chicken plucker every day instead of Daddy. He probably wouldn't even go to work today because it's raining now. Can't a chicken plucker pluck inside?

"Stop that running," Ma says as we run into the kitchen. "The rain is God talking. Surely the two of you ain't scared of the Lord. If you were, you would be good and go on and get yourself ready to go to the mornin' bench tonight."

"We ready, Ma," Twin Luke says, like he

going to eat the shoes right off her feet. Lord knows that I love my ma, but Luke loves her the most. She says he loves her the way he does because he was always a little sickly and she always had to keep him close by her side. He was born with a blue heart, whatever that is. I don't know about the color of Twin Luke's heart. I just know that it belongs to Ma and nobody else.

I guess I will pretend I am a mama's boy so that I can get some extra jelly for my biscuits this morning. Ma makes this jelly and she sells it to the white folks for twenty cents a jar. They buy it as fast as she can make it.

Everybody except Miss Wells. She don't even look at Ma, and she sho' don't want her homemade jelly. That's fine with me, because that leaves more for Twin Luke and me.

Joe Nasty loves it too, but he don't never sit down and eat with us. He says he can't eat at the same table with Filthy Frank. Says his food don't go down right around that man.

"Ma, I promise I am going to be good today. We are going down to that mornin' bench and make you proud tonight," I say, kissing up to her as she spreads extra jelly on my homemade biscuits.

As mad as Ma is with me, she smiles.

"That's good, son. Ma loves you boys."

That's the good thing about my ma. She don't hold no hate in her heart. She forgives us right after she beats our behind. She don't have to forgive Twin Luke much. He ain't got but two beatings in his life. I got about five hundred, but I don't care. I have to be the man around here one day. I don't believe that Filthy Frank will be here forever. I just feel it in my bones.

Ma still smiling.

"Y'all eat your breakfast and clean up your rooms. Ain't no need to go to the fields today, because it's raining to beat the band. If it slows down later on, we will go up to Ma Curry's house to see how she is doing."

Grandma Curry is in her nineties and she live back here in the Neck too. She got white blood like most Neck people. I just don't know which master was her daddy. Ma said if I ever asked her, she will tear my behind up for asking grown folks questions. I been meaning to tell Pattie Mae to do some easedropping to see if she can find out who Grandma Curry daddy is. What I do know is, she got white blood running deep. You can tell by all that long white folks hair she got on her head.

It didn't take us long to finish cleaning our rooms, because they ain't dirty. Ma won't let us keep any room in this house dirty. She says that cleanliness is next to godliness. The question is, Why don't she throw Joe Nasty and Filthy Frank in the hot pot out in the backyard where they clean the dead pigs? I know that Ma is right about being clean, because all the people around here that are dirty ain't baptized. They don't even go to church. When we go to church they be sitting on their nasty front porches looking at us. Miss Elizabeth that lives right down the road is just as nasty as she can be. She ain't swept her front porch in a month of Sundays. Ma said for us to stay away from that house 'cause she ain't got good sense, either. She talks to herself and burn candles on her dead momma's birthday. She like that because her momma died around Christmas twenty years ago and her dying pushed her mind out of place. Don't nobody want to be around her when she playing that church music and crying.

"Ma, we finished our rooms and all the chores are done. The rain done stopped for now. Can we go up to Miss Sarah's house and play with her boys?" I ask as Ma rubs the potbelly stove down with grease. She had that stove all my life and even before that. We don't have much new stuff around here. The only thing that's different is Filthy Frank, and he can leave tonight if he wants to make me happy.

"All right, twins, you can go for a little while. But if you see the clouds coming again, don't go out in the storm. You just stay at Miss Sarah's until it passes over. Frank off today, so we going up to Ma Curry's. You know she don't like being at home in the storm by herself. Joe will meet us there, so we can sit awhile. Frank can pick you all up later if it starts to rain hard."

Pick us up? He need to go to work. I know Filthy Frank don't want to go to my grandma's. He don't want to do nothing that has to do with a Curry.

We kiss Ma. The next thing I know, Twin Luke got his arms around Mr. Filthy Frank's neck, giving him a hug. They are getting too close. I just say bye and run out of the house.

I know Ma really don't want us to go out when it might storm. The flood of 1940 broke people in the Neck from ever going too far away from their house when a storm is coming. It rained and rained for days, according to Ma. It rained until the dam broke and the Roanoke River flooded something awful. They had to call in the National Guard and save the Neck people by boat. The white folks even helped the coloreds. The coloreds helped the whites. Only one person died, and that was a man named Gomez Rawls, who fell out of his boat while he was trying to help save another man.

Ma said she was standing on the roof of Grandma Curry's house and she saw the whole thing. It scared Ma to death. She said she could not sleep for weeks after she saw poor Mr. Rawls float down the raging river.

Miss Sarah is standing on the porch looking at the sky when we reach her house. I don't know how many times Miss Sarah been baptized, but she prays about everything. She is praying right now.

"Thank you, God, for the sunshine as well as the rain." She stops when she sees us.

"Good morning, Miss Sarah. Can your boys come out to play?"

"Good morning, Twin Luke and Twin Leon. I reckon the boys can come out for a while. You sho' ain't going to the fields today. Not when the sky looking so dark and my bones hurting something awfully bad. It's going to rain again. My bones always hurt before a big rain. Mac, you and Tom come out here. The twins here to play."

Mac and Tom sho' act like they glad to get out and play. They almost knock Miss Sarah down running past her. They daddy dead too, but Miss Sarah says she don't want to get married again. I wish Ma could have felt the same way.

Miss Sarah start praying again as soon as we start playing ball. All day we play stickball. As soon as I get ready to hit the ball the tenth time, a loud clap of thunder come from nowhere. It scares Twin Luke and he run onto Miss Sarah's porch.

I swear he ain't got no Curry in him. He got that white Wells blood running too tight in his veins. He still scared of the storm.

Miss Sarah runs out to the porch.

"Come inside, boys, this is going to be a bad storm."

I don't want to stay at Miss Sarah's house. The last time we got caught in a storm here, Filthy Frank didn't come for us until late at night. We had to eat with them, and they ain't that clean either. Miss Sarah gave us a corn biscuit, but she didn't wash the corn. Who ever heard of a corn biscuit anyway? Twin Luke did not eat his, but I was hungry and I ate the whole biscuit and was sick for two days after that. Twin Luke told Joe Nasty, and they teased me for a week.

"Miss Sarah, we thank you, but I think we can make it home before the storm."

Twin Luke just looks at me, because he knows what Ma told us to do.

"Y'all ain't going nowhere," Miss Sarah says

like she is our ma. "Come on in this house."

Mac and Tom follow her inside. As soon as she hit the threshold of her door, I turn to Twin Luke.

"Run, Twin Luke, run!"

I grab his hand and take off running down the path before Miss Sarah can try and stop us.

"Come back here, twins!"

"Don't stop, Twin Luke!"

"Hey! Twin Luke, look at the devil beating his wife!" I yell. We both look at the sun coming out behind the rain. Grandma Curry says the devil is beating his wife when that happens. All of a sudden the sun goes away and the clouds start rolling into one another and it get real dark.

"I'm scared, Twin Leon. I ain't never seen no sky like that before," Twin Luke says.

No sooner than he says those words, the wind starts to blow all the trees to the left, then to the right. Then like God himself grabbing the trees, they just get ripped out of the ground by the roots.

"Run, Twin Luke, run! It's a tornado coming this way!"

I look toward downtown Jackson, and the sky is black as night. Twin Luke running fast as he can. I am running faster, pulling on his white T-shirt. I can see Grandma Curry's house from the road, but it's far away. Twin Luke pulls away from me and start running toward our house.

"Where you going, Twin Luke? Ma is at Grandma's house. Where you going?"

"Our house is closer, so I'm going there!"

"You can go there if you want to, but I am going where Ma is!"

I ain't never run so fast before in my life. My little brother went one way and I went the other.

"Lord, please don't let nothing happen to Twin Luke, because then Ma will surely blame me and I ain't done nothing."

I can't see nothing but a red spot on Grandma Curry's porch, but I know it's Ma's red apron.

"Leoooooonnnnn, where is Luuuuuuuke?" Ma screams as I turn onto the path leading to the house.

"Twin Luke went home, Ma," I say when I reach the back porch, where she is standing with our cousin Wal-Lee and Filthy Frank. Joe Nasty is in the house with Grandma Curry.

"Ain't nobody at that house and the door is locked, child! Lord, have mercy on my child, he is out there in this storm all by his self."

Ma gets down on her knees saying over and over, "Lord have mercy."

I am too scared to get on my knees beside Ma, so I just stand and pray to myself.

Then Ma looks up at me and I know that I'm in trouble. "Now, Leon, you the oldest and I told you to stay at Miss Sarah's house if you saw a storm coming. Get three branches, boy."

"Ma, it's raining and a tornado out there."

"I don't care, get the branches. Frank, get your keys. We got to find Twin Luke."

Cousin Wal-Lee looking like he feel sorry for me. But he can't do nothing much because he ain't got but one arm.

Ma said he lost his arm in a car accident about twenty years ago. He was driving home really fast one night with his arm out of the window when a big truck passed him going in the opposite direction and cut his arm off at the elbow. Wal-Lee passed out and ran his car off the road into the ditch, where Filthy Frank's brother, Mr. Toe Bone, found him bleeding a few hours later. The white man that was driving the truck didn't know he had cut my cousin's arm off until he stopped to get gas up in Norfolk, Virginia. Can you imagine stopping at a gas station and finding an arm stuck on your truck? That white man drove all the way back to the Neck, where he had picked up a load of chickens, and he stopped at every little town in between to find the man who lost his arm. He knew he could not put the arm back on Cousin Wal-Lee, but he wanted to say he was sorry. Ma said he paid all of Wal-Lee doctor bills, although it was not his fault. I think that was a good thing for a white man to do.

I sure wish Cousin Wal-Lee had two arms today. Maybe he would help me out. He turn to Ma.

"Cousin, it's a tornado coming. You can whip the boy later. Let's find Luke."

Filthy Frank ain't saying nothing, because he loves it when I get a whipping. Wal-Lee is my favorite cousin right now. He done saved me from the whipping of my life.

He, Ma, and Filthy Frank try to run to Filthy Frank's car, but the rain coming down so fast and the wind so strong that they just can't stand it and they come back on the porch. Then we all go inside.

Grandma Curry is in the living room praying out loud. I am not to say a word to her because she always say not to bother her while she praying. She is a little bitty woman that ain't as yellow as Ma, but she red from crying right now.

When she gets up off her knees she just look at me.

"Where is your brother?"

"He went home, Grandma Curry."

Joe Nasty in the room too. "Home! Boy, ain't nobody there. He going to get himself killed. The house locked and all the barns are locked too."

He looks at Ma and then back at me. "I got to find him."

He gets Filthy Frank's keys and heads for the door. When he opens it the door break away from the house and fly into the air.

"Great God Almighty! Everyone run," he shouts.

Joe Nasty picks Grandma Curry up and we

all run and get in the pantry with the smoked hams that are hanging from the ceiling. I think the storm is going to blow us all clean to Heaven, and ain't nobody saved but Ma and Grandma Curry.

God is with us, even though Filthy Frank is in the pantry too. When I look up, the hams are gone and so is the ceiling. We are looking at the sky as rain is falling down on us.

Grandma Curry shouts over the wind, "Don't worry, Lemuel, Twin Luke is all right. I ain't seen and I ain't felt no death. He all right." Grandma Curry always know when death is coming. If she say he is alive, then he is alive.

I feel like my twin ain't dead, but I can't stop crying to save my life. But Ma just fine after that, because she trust her mother-in-law like she trust God. Ma says that Grandma Curry always been good to her, and she got the gift. Grandma Curry can sense certain things. Like the time when Daddy got killed.

She knew something was wrong long before the law came to tell us that Daddy was dead. She said she was sound asleep the night Daddy was killed and the next thing she knew she was sitting straight up in her bed. She said she saw him floating in the water as plain as day. The next morning the law came and gave her the bad news.

Ma says that maybe Grandma ain't just got the gift to see things, she got the gift of love.

Ma says she married Daddy when she was nothing but a child, and Grandma Curry helped take care of them until they could get on their feet. Grandma Curry and Grandma Ella liked each other and loved their grandchildren. When Ma started having labor pains with Joe Nasty, they ran Daddy outside and together they brought Joe Nasty into the world. So he was born right here in this use-to-be house and he stayed here until Ma and Daddy moved into Mr. Wells's house after Grandma Ella died. Now this birth house don't have no roof.

Filthy Frank opens the door and step out of the pantry. Then we hear a voice.

"Ma, it's me!"

It's Twin Luke. He is alive! I don't have to live out the rest of my days without my twin.

Ma runs past Filthy Frank and hugs Twin Luke so hard that he has to pull away so he can breathe.

Grandma is praying again and Joe Nasty and Wal-Lee trying to put whatever paper they can find over Grandma Curry's belongings. Filthy Frank doing what he always do. Nothing!

When Ma stop hugging Twin Luke, she starts to fuss at us both.

"Twin Luke, take your brother and go and get six branches. Braid them yourself and come back in this house."

I can't believe it. The roof is off of Grandma Curry's house and Luke almost died, but Ma is still going to whip us. Joe Nasty and Filthy Frank glad we getting a whipping and Cousin Wal-Lee know he can't save us now.

Two whippings in one week! Now Ma and Grandma Curry packing up her things to come live with us. Filthy Frank don't want her with us, but Ma says too bad, and Grandma is sleeping in the room with me and Twin Luke for now.

I am glad to be home. Our house damaged too, but we still got a roof.

"Go to bed, twins. Ain't no need to go to the mornin' bench tonight. The way things are looking, you won't be saved this year. Not with your hard heads."

WEDNESDAY

MA SENT US TO BED without supper last night. Now we have to stay home and wash down every wall in the house as punishment for leaving Miss Sarah's in the storm. It's still too wet to go in the 'bacco field, and Joe Nasty say the tornado blew half the 'bacco away. I hope it blew clean to New York and we will be done working for the year. Then I can go back to school before September. I will learn enough to keep my brain sharp until cotton-picking time. In the fall we still have to come home early to pick cotton, but we don't have to stay out of school as much.

There ain't nothing I would like more than to get a high school diploma from Creecy like the one Pattie Mae going to get.

Twin Luke ain't said a word to me all day. I don't care because he ain't talking about nothing no way. He real mad because the county fair is set up in Weldon and tonight is boys' night. Filthy Frank got tickets from his job for us to go. I guess the chicken house is good for something. Joe Nasty says the storm didn't blow the fair away because they had a radio and knew the storm was coming. They had time to nail stuff down and get it together for safekeeping. We have a radio but it's broke, so God told us the storm was coming.

I have been saving pennies all summer for candy and a toy from the fair. Now I might not get anything. Just another sore behind. Maybe Grandma Curry can talk Ma into letting us go. In the meantime, I will mention that it's boys' night when I finish the walls. Before I can say anything, though, Filthy Frank announces that we are going to the county fair before church tonight.

"No, they are not!" Ma shouts.

"Now, honey, my boss gave me these tickets and they need to go!" He says it real meanlike and look at my ma.

Ma do not say another word. Joe Nasty give Filthy Frank the look of death for hollering at Ma, but he wants to go too, so he ain't going to listen to Ma go on about this one. I know a fight is coming. I just know it's coming. Ma so mad she stay at home.

I might start liking Filthy Frank after all. Well, let's not go that far. I like him tonight because he taking me to the fair.

This fair is something else. All the cotton candy in the world is right here. All the people from the Neck, Rich Square, and Jackson are here. The Potecasi people are here too. I don't see them much since they got they own school. The Potecasi people don't look white like us. They mostly look like Indians. Ma said the word "Potecasi" means "river divided" or "parted water." She says when she use to chop 'bacco over in Potecasi, they used to find Indian arrowheads all over the fields. Folks say the whole town is a burial ground for the Indians that were killed by the white people who took their land. So some of the people left are pure Indians, or they look like they are. Potecasi is one of the few towns that still has its old name. Rich white folks changed all the other towns' names. Conway used to be called Kirby, but the name was changed to Conway after they brought the railroad. Folks believe that Woodland was called something else but was changed to Woodland after slave owner James Wood. But Potecasi is Potecasi.

As soon as we park the car, Joe Nasty finds his girlfriend, Margie, who is from Potecasi. I like her because anytime we can get a ride, she let us go fishing with her over at Potecasi Creek. She is definitely related to the Indians, with her dark hair and pretty skin. She is skinny, but Lord she is pretty. And she smells like peaches. She better be glad she was not in the storm, because the wind would have blown her away. I wonder why she like Joe Nasty so much? She go to school. Joe Nasty don't. She takes a bath. Joe Nasty don't.

They looking at a gorilla in a cage. I ain't never seen no gorilla before. Of course Twin Luke is scared of the gorilla and everything else breathing out here that ain't human.

Filthy Frank done found his way over to the card table. I should have known he had his own reason he was breaking his neck to come out to the fair. He wanted to gamble. I wonder if Ma knows about this? Something tells me that Ma don't know a lot that Filthy Frank like to do, and look at all them women hanging around him like he a piece of candy.

The man in charge of the gorilla is talking

on a bullhorn. He says he will give any man at the fair twenty dollars to fight the gorilla with their bare hands for three minutes.

Before I could tell Twin Luke, "Ain't nobody that crazy," our brother Joe Nasty raised his hand.

"I'll fight the gorilla," he says real loud!

His girlfriend looks at him like she done seen two ghosts.

"Why, Joe, that gorilla will kill you," she says.

"We will see about that."

The gorilla man knows a fool when he sees one.

"We have a fighter here, folks. What's your name, sir?"

"Joe, Joe Curry!"

As soon as Joe Nasty says he will fight the gorilla, people start clapping, laughing, screaming, and hollering, and Filthy Frank comes running over to see what is going on.

Right there in front of the whole county, Filthy Frank tells Joe Nasty he is not fighting the gorilla, and then Joe Nasty does what I have wanted to do for a long time. "You ain't my daddy, Frank."

There, I am a happy twin!

Joe Nasty just walks into the cage and looks at the gorilla.

The gorilla is wearing a catcher's mask and boxing gloves. Joe Nasty figures that the gorilla can't bite or scratch him, so this is going to be easy money.

My Lord! Joe Nasty done hit the gorilla.

I don't think Joe Nasty remembers anything after that.

The gorilla picks him up and throws him up in the cage like a ball. Then the gorilla slings Joe Nasty by one arm around and around his head. Then he drops him to the ground.

"Stop! You're going to kill my big brother!" Twin Luke screams.

"Stop this right now!" Filthy Frank shouts to the gorilla man.

I think the whole thing is pretty funny myself.

Finally, after Joe Nasty's girlfriend faints, the gorilla man shoots a sleeper dart into the gorilla, and down he goes.

When Joe Nasty wakes up, Filthy Frank tries to take him to the hospital, but Joe Nasty will not go. He keeps screaming something about where is his money until the white man pays him. He won't go to the hospital, so we go home.

We are trying to get home in time for church. Ma is waiting for us at the door. She already knew what happen with Joe Nasty and the gorilla because White Cousin was at the fair and he went home and told his daddy and his daddy came and told Ma right away.

For two people who act like they ain't related, they sure do tell each other everything. You see, it ain't just Twin Luke and White Cousin bringing and carrying bones. That's what Miss Babe say about folks that tell each other everything. She call it carrying bones. I call it talking too much.

Ma does not even ask Joe Nasty if he is okay. She looks him up and down while he getting out of the car, and then she says the wrong thing.

"You just as crazy as your daddy when he had his mind made up, boy!"

All of Joe Nasty's pain goes away. He stands up and looks Ma square in her eyes.

"Ma, if you want me to stay under your roof, don't ever say another bad word about my daddy."

I know Ma is sorry the minute she looks into Joe Nasty's eyes. She puts her arms around her oldest boy and helps him to bed. Then she come in the kitchen and looks at Twin Luke, me, and Filthy Frank. She just looks at us for a long time.

"Frank, do you hate my child enough to let him kill himself?"

"Like you said, he crazy like his daddy."

Those words never reach Joe Nasty's ear, but Grandma Curry hears him.

"Frank, you may be married to my son's wife, but you have no right to say things against my boy." Grandma Curry says what she wants to say, but she never looks up from making her tea.

That scares Ma, because she knows about that Smith & Wesson.

Filthy Frank walks out and Ma turns to us.

"Twins, why on earth did you let this happen?"

For the first time, I want to agree with Filthy Frank and tell Ma that Joe Nasty is crazy, but I don't want another whipping. I am tired of whippings.

"Ma, we tried to stop him, but he wouldn't listen."

"You know you ain't going to the mornin' bench tonight. Get ready for church, but you better not go down that aisle. Y'all can't tell Reverend Webb nothing about how good you been. Now get dressed."

I can't believe Ma. It's a shame and a

disgrace that we can't be saved tonight because Joe Nasty is a crazy sinner. I got enough of my own sins to pay for. Why do I have to pay for his, too?

Church is full tonight. It's full of folks who want to get saved, because they are running out of nights to go to the mornin' bench. If they do not go to the mornin' bench tonight, they only got Thursday night and Friday night left to meet their Lord.

Tomorrow night Twin Luke and me are going to the mornin' bench for sure.

5

THURSDAY

COME MORNIN' Twin Luke still ain't saying much to me. He must think this is the worst week of his life. It has been pretty bad for two people who are trying to get saved.

When we get to the 'bacco field to gather the little 'bacco that is left, we stay next to each other all day. I know that Twin Luke is staying close to me because he wants to keep an eye on me to keep me out of trouble. We are doing fine until White Cousin shows up with his mess.

"Hey, Luke, how that crazy gorilla-fighting brother of yours doing?" Then White Cousin starts walking toward Twin Luke and laughing. Something comes over Twin Luke that I ain't never seen before.

"Shut up, White Cousin!"

He called White Cousin "White Cousin" for the first time in his face.

Twin Luke looks White Cousin right in the face.

"Leave my brother alone," I say, thinking that Twin Luke needs some help. I am wrong, because he said it again.

"Shut up, White Cousin."

This shocked poor White Cousin and he run off crying.

White Cousin don't have to tell his daddy so that his daddy will tell Ma. Twin Luke goes home and tells on himself.

Ma don't say much. She don't even tell him to get three branches or nothing. Something is wrong, and I know it has something to do with Filthy Frank, because he ain't talking either. They act like this after they argue.

Finally, Ma says, "Get dressed, twins. You both going to the church tonight. You ain't going to the mornin' bench, but you going to church. Whatever your sins are, tell God, because I am tired. Tell God, children."

When we get to church, it is filled with people again. All just waiting to see who is going to the mornin' bench.

Two boys that I don't know get up and go down to the mornin' bench looking scared to death.

Then a girl gets up, and I know her. That's Pattie Mae. She looks so pretty all dressed up. I ain't seen her in a while. Because we ain't going back to school until we finish with tobacco. We spent a lot of time together when Cousin Buddy left.

Cousin Buddy has been back twice since the whole mess with the white woman. He was here for Cousin Braxton's funeral, and he came back when they had a trial for the men who tried to hang him. That same day they had a trial for Cousin Buddy, but they let him go. They knew in their hearts that he never tried to harm that white woman. Ma says that one hundred years from now they will still be talking about Buddy Bush.

Pattie Mae was really sad. She is one pretty sight to see. If we was not kinfolks, I would marry her the day we turn eighteen.

I whisper to Ma that I want to marry Pattie Mae one day, and she tells me to shut my mouth talking about marrying kinfolks. I remind her that Cousin Buddy was adopted by Pattie Mae folks when his family died in an accident on the 'bacco farm. We just call Pattie Mae cousin, but she ain't our blood kin.

Ma just looks at me like I am some kind of crazy and say, "Cousins are cousins in these parts, and that's your cousin, boy. Now, hush, and listen to Reverend Webb."

"Well, I guess I will just have to leave these parts," I whisper to Twin Luke.

Just before Reverend Webb get ready to close the doors of the church, Twin Luke looks at Ma and start crying.

"Ma, please let me go down to the mornin' bench tonight."

She has such a soft heart for Twin Luke.

"Go on, son. God knows your heart."

She don't even look at me because she knows that God knows mine, too. She know that God know I don't want to get baptized in the name of the Father, the Son, and nobody else. I just want to go home and shoot marbles.

Twin Luke goes right down there and sits beside my Pattie Mae.

I still ain't going tonight.

Reverend Webb looks down at Twin Luke, Pattie Mae, and the boys that I don't know, and smiles.

"Well, I see we have Li'l Luke coming to meet his savior tonight."

I can't see Twin Luke's face, but I know he is crying again.

"Little Luke, are you ready to be saved?"

My little brother stands up and say, "Yes, sir, I am, I am ready!"

Reverend Webb knows everybody in the county, and he goes down the mornin' bench and asks each and every person if they are ready. They all say yes.

The church breaks into song.

Ma cries something awful.

Grandma sings, "Have you been baptized?" and the whole church joins in.

When we get back into Filthy Frank's car, Ma does what she does best. She fusses all the way home.

"See, Twin Leon, you know you should be good and you could have gone to the mornin' bench too."

What is Ma talking about? I am not the one who called White Cousin "White Cousin."

She need to fuss at Filthy Frank, who sat

in the car mad and didn't get any religion
tonight.

I am so glad when we get home.

I am so glad when we all get in bed.

Ma's mouth is finally closed.

6

FRIDAY

TODAY IS THE DAY I am going to do the right thing with God and get myself to the mornin' bench. Today is the day I will say no wrong, do no wrong, and think no wrong. Today I will start my journey to the water on Sunday morning.

"Luke, wake up. Today is the day I am going to the mornin' bench."

"Twin Leon, leave me be, I am trying to sleep a little. . . ." Then I hear Ma, and it sound like she is crying.

"Hush, Twin Luke, I think Ma is in the kitchen crying."

I jump out of bed. Luke chases after me, and we run to Joe Nasty's room. He is still asleep from all the medicine the doctor gave him for his gorilla fight.

"Joe Nasty, wake up. Ma in the kitchen crying. Ma crying, Joe Nasty. Now, wake up."

Before I can say it again, Joe Nasty is on his feet, out the door, and in the kitchen.

"What's wrong, Ma, why are you crying?"

Ma don't say a word.

She lifts her head from the table and my blood rush to my head. Ma's face is filled with tears. She don't have to say a word. Filthy Frank done something to Ma.

"Let's go, Twin Leon," Joe Nasty says real low and slow.

My big brother didn't have to say that. I am getting my shoes.

I'm never going to make it to the mornin' bench and I will never get baptized, I'm thinking as I get Daddy's shotgun from under Joe Nasty's bed.

Twin Luke standing here crying his eyes out. He took up for Joe Nasty when White Cousin called him "gorilla-fighting brother" in the fields, but somebody bothers Ma and he crying.

"Ain't no time for crying, Twin Luke. What happen to you, Ma?" I ask, but she ain't talking.

Grandma is a woman who knows how to mind her business, but not today.

"Frank left your ma last night because he don't want me staying here. He took all her money. He was trying to get something from under the bed mattress until he saw my Smith & Wesson."

All the man in Joe Nasty just rise up like the water down in the river right after a big rain.

"Oh, he shouldn't have done that," he says as he put on his shoes. "Where is he, Ma?"

She don't answer. Joe Nasty grabs Ma by the arm.

"Lord, children, stop!" she screams.

Joe Nasty can't talk now. His mouth is all twisted with anger. He tries to walk out the door, but Ma is blocking him in.

"You my oldest boy, and you better not leave this land. Frank ain't scared of you, and he will hurt you like white folks did your daddy."

For the first time, Ma admits that she know they murdered Daddy.

"He halfway to New York by now. I made the mistake of marrying him. I will not have my boys going to jail. Let him go."

"Filthy Frank made the mistake, Ma. Not you. Now, move."

Grandma ain't trying to stop us. She is just as capable of going after Filthy Frank as we are.

"I buried the only man I ever loved. Your daddy. I married Frank because I thought you boys needed a daddy. Now, don't go out and do nothing crazy."

Joe Nasty ain't listening to Ma.

"Ma, the only person crazy around here was Filthy Frank."

Me and Joe Nasty put the gun down and walk out the door.

Joe Nasty turns to my brother and says, "Twin Luke, you stay here with Ma and Grandma."

Ma follows us all the way down the path, crying and screaming for us to come back.

But there ain't no turning back. We are going to find Filthy Frank and get Ma's money back.

The first place we stop is the chicken house to see if Filthy Frank had the nerve to go to work. His boss man don't want no trouble.

"Frank ain't been here," he yells through the locked door.

We leave and go into town. All day we look for Filthy Frank. Ain't nobody in Jackson seen him. At least no one is saying they saw him. It don't take long for word to get around town that we are out looking for "Filthy No Good for Nothing Frank."

Come evening, folks start coming to us and telling us to go home. Then folks start going to the Neck and telling Ma that they saw us. Within an hour they tell us to go home because Ma is there crying and getting sick with worry about us.

Ma was right. Filthy Frank ain't nowhere to be found.

Joe Nasty and me walk all the way home. When we get there, Ma and everybody else is gone. She left a note on the door: "We at church."

I can't believe that Ma went to church when the whole town know her husband stole her money and left her. But she got so much grace that she don't have no shame.

We don't even change clothes; we just go to the church to find our ma.

When I walk into the church with Joe Nasty, everybody looks back at us. Ma looks back and screams, "Oh, thank you, Jesus!"

Grandma Curry dancing around the church like she got the Holy Ghost. She dancing like she forgot that she is ninety years old.

Twin Luke is letting out his girl tears.

With our dirty clothes, we go to Ma. She has hurt in her face, but I can tell her heart is okay now that her boys are back safe. I stand there a few minutes, and then Ma looks down at the mornin' bench; then she looks at me.

I pull away from her and walk toward the mornin' bench. The mornin' bench that Ma said would set me free. If I could have found Filthy Frank, God knows I would be sitting on a jail bench and not this mornin' bench.

Reverend Webb looks down at me, seeing as I'm the only person on the mornin' bench.

"Welcome to the Lord's house, son. Are you ready to be saved?"

There is no turning back.

"Yes, sir, I'm ready."

Miss Lou Value gets the Holy Ghost when I say that. She is Ma's friend from grade school. She starts to sing.

"Will you be ready when Jesus comes? Will you be ready to answer the call?"

I sing back, "Yes, I will be ready."

Miss Lou Value screams, "Lord, I will be ready when Jesus comes!"

Twin Luke joins in, and he and Miss Lou Value do a few notes together.

7

SATURDAY

MA FINALLY TOLD US that Filthy Frank ran out of the house in the middle of the night and left his gold watch when he saw Grandma's Smith & Wesson and he ain't never getting it back. He had it under the mattress and he should have been paying bills with the watch money, so Ma says we might as well put it to good use. Ma ain't spoke to Miss Rose in years, but she walked to her house this mornin' and asked her to buy the watch. She gave Ma a whole $150 for that watch. We are all getting new suits for the baptism. I think I will get a blue one and I know if I get a blue suit, then Twin Luke will want blue too.

Ma says as soon as we can get a ride today, we're going up to Sears Roebuck in Rocky Mount to get our suits. I ain't never been to Sears Roebuck before. I ain't never been to Rocky Mount. We get most of our clothes up at the thrift store in Jackson. Daddy always hated that store, but it was the best he could do. But whenever he could, he would go to Kennedy's and buy us an outfit that was brand-new. Filthy Frank thought that the old thrift store was good enough for us, but he would buy his clothes at Sears Roebuck. I remember one time we needed boots, and he said he would get each of us a pair on payday. Payday came three times before he came home with a box from the thrift store that had "$2.00" written on the side. It was filled with ice skates. Filthy Frank said to just cut the blades off and we could wear them for boots.

Ma cried herself to sleep that night.

That's how we found out for sure that Cousin Buddy was still in Harlem.

Pattie Mae wrote her uncle and told him about the ice skates that Filthy Frank brought home to us, and Cousin Buddy mailed us all pairs of boots in a box with no return address, but the box was postmarked New York.

Ma said that was nobody but Buddy Bush looking out for his cousin's children. Ma walked all the way from the Neck to Rehobeth Road to tell Miss Babe to tell Buddy Bush thank you. Ma didn't want to write Miss Babe a letter because Ma thought the post office opened every piece of mail that Miss Babe had gotten for a year. That's sheriff's orders. The law just wanted to keep up with Cousin Buddy's coming and goings, like it was their business.

We are getting dressed and praying that someone would come along and give us a ride to Rocky Mount. Ma said she would pay them a dollar. God hear Ma because someone is knocking on the door now. I answer and it is Mr. Arthur standing on the porch.

What in the world does he want? I think when I see his white face, the face that looks just like Ma's. He don't never come on the porch. He just sits in the truck and yells for his rent or yell to Ma how we beat White Cousin.

"Is your mother home, child?"

At least he don't call me boy. I ain't in the mood for white folks' mess today.

"Yes, sir, she here."

Ma comes to the door.

"How can I help you, Arthur?"

"I would like to come in, if it's all right."

Ma turns and looks at me.

"Boy, have you been messing with Arthur's boy again?"

"No, ma'am, I haven't touched him lately."

"He ain't done nothing wrong. I came by to see about you," Mr. Arthur said.

"See about me? Why is that?"

"Well, the folks in town called me and told me what Frank done and all, and I don't like that. Miss Lou Value told me that you needed a ride to Rocky Mount, and I thought you could use my old pickup to drive yourself up there."

I can't believe my ears.

"Why, thank you, Arthur, I appreciate it. I will take good care of your truck, and I will have it back by dark."

"Ain't no need to hurry. Why don't you just use it for church tomorrow?"

"That would be nice. Awfully nice, Arthur. Thank you."

"You don't have to thank me. Keep it as long as you like."

Tears start to roll down Ma's face as she reaches her hand out to shake Mr. Arthur's hand. Her brother's hand.

He don't take Ma's hand. He put his arms around her and hold her like he loves her. Ma hugs her white brother back. They know they kin.

They do love each other. This is what Ma meant when she said that prayer and getting saved changes things.

I don't believe he had ever touched a colored person before.

When he let Ma go, he is as red as a beet.

"Have a good time in Rocky Mount and church tomorrow."

Ma thinks for a minute, then she say something she has no business saying without asking Reverend Webb.

"Why don't you come to the baptism tomorrow?"

"Well, now, I don't know if I could feel quite welcome, but I thank you for the invite."

He don't give Ma a chance to ask him again, because he do not want to come to no colored church. Her brother leaves as fast as he came.

I look out the window as he gets into the car with his son, who followed him up to the house to give him a ride if Ma said she would use the old truck. Mr. Arthur know White Cousin ain't old enough to be driving. I bet Miss Rose don't know Mr. Arthur is leaving that truck with Ma.

They wave at us. We wave back.

When we are pulling out of the driveway, Miss Fossie run to the truck and tells us that Filthy Frank is sitting in the county jail. Miss Fossie says that Ma's white brother was so mad about him stealing Ma's money that he ask the sheriff to arrest him. It turns out that when he left Ma's house, Filthy Frank had stopped at the theater to get some more money from his cousin, Guy Boone, who cleans the theater. He couldn't get far with $40.00, and he couldn't come back for his watch. The sheriff knew he had folks in Rich Square, and they waited for him right there at the theater. The same theater where they arrested Cousin Buddy in front of in 1947. The only difference is, Cousin Buddy hadn't done nothing wrong. Filthy Frank, on the other hand, made the worst mistake of his life. He now has something in common with Cousin Buddy, though. He can't stay in these parts ever again.

If Cousin Buddy tries to come back, the white folks will get him. If Filthy Frank stays after his trial, I will do the honors. He ain't going to steal from my ma and stay here.

Filthy Frank ain't worth nothing, but that watch money got us new suits, new shoes, and new underwear from Sears Roebuck. Ma bought herself a new dress and a suit for Joe Nasty, who stayed home with Grandma Curry. Ma knows better than to buy Grandma Curry anything with that man's watch money. Me, I don't care at this point about Filthy Frank, so long as I never see him again.

After we spent most of Filthy Frank's watch money, Ma put the rest in her bra for a rainy day. It is not much. Just enough to help me remember that Filthy Frank's gone for good.

8

SUNDAY

THE SUN ROSE EARLY this morning. It's kind of like God is telling me that today is going to be a special day. Ma is up early and the kitchen smells like blueberries. Surely Ma is not cooking blueberry muffins. She usually freezes the blueberries to save for Christmastime. When they thaw out, she drops them in the homemade dough that's waiting in the muffin pans that she found in this house when she and my daddy moved in after Grandma Ella died.

"Wake up, Twin Luke. I think Ma is cooking blueberry muffins!" That woke Twin Luke right up.

"But it ain't Christmas," he says.

Then Twin Luke smells the berries and jumps out of bed.

We make it to the kitchen at the same time.

"Good morning, Ma."

"Good morning, twins. Guess what I'm cooking this morning?"

Grandma Curry walks in already dressed for church before I can answer Ma.

"Well, grandchilluns, looks like today is the day for you all to make your ma and daddy proud," Grandma Curry says.

Grandma always talk about her son just like he still on this earth. He was her only child and she just ain't never got over his death. Most of all, Miss Babe says, she ain't never got past the thought of someone murdering him over fifteen dollars.

"We are happy that we are making you proud, Grandma," Twin Luke says.

I'm in such a good mood I say, "Me too, Grandma."

It was a wonderful breakfast. Joe Nasty even got up early to take a bath. And he sat at the table and ate with us like folks with good sense do.

I think Twin Luke is going to shine a hole in his shoes. They look good, and he shines my penny loafers.

We put on baptism clothes and carry our church clothes in a bag. Ma holds on to our suits. We will change into our suits after we go down in the water. When we are all ready, we climb into my white uncle's truck and head down the road. Ma, Grandma, and Joe Nasty get in the front. Joe Nasty do not want to drive his white uncle's truck, so Ma doing the driving. Twin Luke and me climb onto the back and sit in the two wood chairs that Ma made us put back here. We don't get far before we see Miss Sarah walking with Tom and Mac. They got baptized last year. They mighty dressed up this morning, even if their house is nasty.

Just like I know she would, Ma stops.

"Y'all need a ride to Branches Chapel this morning?"

Miss Sarah knows how to mind her business, and she don't say one word about Ma driving her white brother's truck. She just smiles and says, "Why, I don't mind if we do. Hop on, boys."

Joe Nasty gets out of the front and let Miss Sarah sit with Ma and Grandma Curry. Ma starts down the road again, and before we can say good morning to the boys, Ma is stopping again. This time for Mr. Rowbell King and his wife, Miss Rebecca. They don't have no children. Mr. Rowbell helps Miss Rebecca onto the back, and I get up to give her my chair.

We almost make it out of the Neck when

Ma spots Ole Man Jefferson and his wife, Miss Maggie. We only have room for Miss Maggie to sit in a chair after Twin Luke gets up. Ole Man Jefferson sits on the bed of the truck with us.

Lord, we have a time on the back of that truck.

Miss Maggie says she can remember when Branches Chapel Church was built. She says before that, folks had church outside under a tree.

"Miss Maggie, how old were you when you got baptized?" I ask her without caring if Twin Luke tells Ma later that I was getting in grown folks' business.

"Son, I am eighty-two years old. I have been saved for seventy years. I remember just like it was yesterday when I went down in the water. Reverend Webb's granddaddy was the preacher back then. He preached a good sermon that morning. When he was done, we all followed him down to the riverbank. I took going down in that water real serious. After that day, I never said another cuss word. I know I have made a mistake or two. I just try not to lie and I ain't never stole from nobody. So when you go down in that water, you come up new, if you right with God."

After that Miss Maggie don't say another word. She starts moving back and forth in the chair that Twin Luke let her sit in, and she sings all the way to church, "Will you be ready to answer the call? Have you been faithful to Jesus at all?"

Everyone join in and sing all the way to the churchyard. Ma parks the truck right beside Mr. Charlie's car. I sure want to see how pretty Pattie Mae Sheals is today. She always rides to church with Mr. Charlie. They are members of Chapel Hill Church and they don't have church today.

Last week I asked Ma why Pattie Mae joining our church. She said it ain't my business, but then I overheard her say to Grandma Curry that Pattie Mae wanted to be a member of Branches because that was Cousin Buddy's church.

Rules can be broken. Pattie Mae somehow talked her ma into breaking the rules.

When we get inside, Ma pushes me and Twin Luke in our backs so that we will go on down to the front row. Down to the mornin' bench. There is Pattie Mae wrapped in a white cotton dress with something dark under it so that boys like me can't get a peek when she get wet. Her hair is all wrapped up too. I am in heaven.

Reverend Webb preaches about staying near the cross. Then Miss Lou Value sings.

When it is time to go down to the water, Reverend Webb says, "Church, it is time to go to the water. When we finish, we will get the children dressed and come back for a second service and an early dinner. Church, we going to take our time walking

down to the water today. I want you to take
your time walking behind Miss Maggie.
She is the oldest member of the church.
She was baptized here seventy years ago.
Stand up, Miss Maggie."

Miss Maggie stands up and her oldest boy,
Whisper, who lives over in Woodland, walks
her to the side door, where Reverend Webb
joins them. Ole Man Jefferson is a deacon, so
he got to walk with the other deacons.

We follow Reverend Webb.

It is a beautiful mornin'.

A couple women folks shout along the way.
They shouting because we are going to be
saved in just a few minutes.

The men folks help them up when they fall
due to the Holy Ghost taking over.

Grandma Curry got a nice voice, and she
and Miss Novella, who live on Rehobeth
Road, get to singing a new song, and the line
of folks can't take it no more. They shout all
over Branches Chapel churchyard.

When the shouting is over, the women put their hats back on and the men try to pretend their backs ain't hurting from picking up the big women folks.

Joe Nasty is laughing at all the carrying on. Ma is going to get him when we get home.

When we get to the riverbank, you would have thought Jesus Christ himself was waiting. Ma gets to shouting all over the place. I don't know what is going on. Then I look up and see four white folks. It is Mr. Arthur, his wife, Miss Ann, Miss Rose, and White Cousin. I don't know if a white man has ever stepped on the grounds of this land since coloreds built this church here. I will ask Grandma Curry later. She knows everything about Branches. She told me that the land was given to colored folks after the Civil War. Grandma said that during slavery, coloreds could only go to church service on Sunday evening at the white folks' church after the whites was done. Some of the white folks would let the coloreds go to church with them and sit in the balcony or in the back. Grandma Curry said that most slaves preferred the evening service away from the white folks. It was there they planned their escapes after they thanked God for keeping them alive all week.

But today is different. The Wellses are here because they want to do the right thing by Ma. Something broke in Mr. Arthur's heart when he found out that Filthy Frank hurt Ma. Maybe he knows he should have protected Ma. Maybe he knows he looks just like her. Ma don't go over to her white brother. He nods at her and she nods back. White Cousin, who I think I will call Little Arthur from now on, waves.

I wave back.

Yes, I will be ready when Jesus comes.

The girls go down in the water first. One by one they hold on to Reverend Webb and the man who is helping him. Deacon Jacobs usually helps, but today this man with a white beard helps. I can't see much of his face because he is all wrapped in white too.

"Twin Luke, do you want to go first?" I ask.

Twin Luke ain't scared today. He don't even answer me, he just steps up to the water. He smiles real big, just like Pattie Mae had done when the man in the water helping Reverend Webb whisper something in his ear.

Now it's my turn.

When my feet first touch the water, it don't feel like regular water. I feel bad about beating up White Cousin and taking the extra cookies from Ma's cookie jar. I even feel bad for wanting to beat some sense into Filthy Frank.

I can hear Ma crying. Grandma Curry talking out loud to Daddy like he is here.

"Son, your boys, Twin Luke and Twin Leon, are getting baptized this morning. Praise the Lord." Joe Nasty ain't saying a word.

When the big man all wrapped in white puts his hand on my back, Reverend Webb stands over me and says, "Son, I baptize you in the name of the Father, the Son, and the Holy Ghost." Just before the big man lowers me into the water, he whispers in my ear, "It's me, Cousin Buddy."

Down I go.

I am saved for sure.

Author's Note

WHEN I was a little girl growing up on Rehobeth Road in Rich Square, North Carolina, everything was handled according to your age and the season. You did not cook the collard greens until after the first frost. You did not wear white until after Easter Sunday, and you could not get baptized until you were twelve years old.

The summer of 1973 I celebrated my twelfth birthday, knowing that in August I would go down in the holy water at Chapel Hill Baptist Church and be baptized. I was spared the river, because the church had a baptizing pool under the pulpit. Being the ninth of ten children, I had watched all my older siblings go down to the mornin' bench to tell Reverend Wiggins that they had accepted God and they wanted to get baptized. It was more than a religious ceremony. It was a family tradition.

During the week of the baptism, we attended the church revival at least three nights. On one of those three nights you were supposed to go down front and sit in the front pew—the *mornin' bench.*

This book is the story about the mornin' bench and two little boys who are very much like my two brothers Larry and Leon, who we called Ben and Boosie. My brothers are not twins, but they have always been two peas in a pod. Ben is the oldest. As a child he was filled with mischief and excitement. Boosie was quiet and followed Ben's every move. They were not fighters like the boys in this book. But they did everything else under the sun and God only knows how they made it to the mornin' bench. The twins in this book are a combination of all the little boys who lived on Rehobeth Road and in the Neck. They are like all the little boys who got baptized when they turned twelve years old.

Acknowledgments

My Earth Angels

Maless Moses
Eric L. Goins
Barbara, James, and Chris Lucas
April, Jamil, and Jala Marshall
Daniel and Courtney Moses
Johnny, Ronetta, Tarsula, and Keidra Moses
Scarlett and Al Spivey
Byron and Andrea Joyner
Larry, Larry Jr., Melanie, and Rhonda Moses
Leon, Iris, Leon Jr., and Leonynce Moses
Ted, Loraine, Malcolm, and TJ Stewart
Gayle Moses
Jackie, Larry, Jada, and Jasmine Marshall
Kim, Elliott, Trey, and Eric Abnatha
Wanda and Lauren Linden
Jordan Francais
Corteney D. Bradley
Sylvine Blackwell
The Goins/Rowell/Pots Family
April Russell
Myra Dixon
The 100 Black Men of Atlanta, Inc.
Jonathan Lyons
Lucia Smeal
Sheila Frazier
Barbara Austin and Paul Benjamin
Edward Necarsulmer IV
Emma Dryden
Dick Gregory